LAST RITES

Final Confession

PAUL BOUCHARD

iUniverse LLC
Bloomington

LAST RITES
FINAL CONFESSION

This is a work of fiction. All of the characters, names, incidents, organizations, and dialogue in this novel are either the products of the author's imagination or are used fictitiously.

iUniverse books may be ordered through booksellers or by contacting:

iUniverse LLC
1663 Liberty Drive
Bloomington, IN 47403
www.iuniverse.com
1-800-Authors (1-800-288-4677)

ISBN: 978-1-4917-2118-6 (sc)
ISBN: 978-1-4917-2119-3 (e)

Library of Congress Control Number: 2014901866

Printed in the United States of America.

iUniverse rev. date: 03/04/2014

For Stephen King, my biggest inspiration.

October 2012

Friday

I'm dying. I know I am. Writing's on the wall. The big C—cancer. Of the lung variety. Of the terminal variety. At least that's what the doctor told me just a couple of days ago. He gave me some six months to live. I've been battling cancer for the last three years now. Chemo did its thing for some time, but it wasn't enough. It'll be game over soon.

"Too advanced to operate; spread in both lungs." That's what he said. Not good of course. If life is a baseball game, then I'm in the last inning with no extra innings in sight.

Name's Glenn Greenwood, born Gilles Boisvert forty-seven years ago, right here in this small town of Frenchville, Maine, population fifteen hundred and declining. I changed my name when I was seventeen to anglicize it, to make it easier to pronounce. Translates directly to English, actually.

I'm now sitting in a rocking chair in my tiny room at the St. John Valley Nursing Home. What can I say— I'm like everybody else here, on my last legs, relegated to kicking the bucket soon.

But there is a twist to my terminal cancer predicament— that is, Father LaBrie's recent visit. He's the parish Catholic priest, and he visits this nursing home weekly. Less than an hour ago, he saw me and we chatted.

"Glenn, I'll administer your last rites tomorrow, but before I do, I want to take you for a short ride, a short trip. I can also administer the sacrament of confession when you want it."

Confession doesn't bother me, even though I haven't done it in years, maybe a decade. But this "I want to take you for a short ride" comment gets me wondering. I asked,

"Where to, Father?" but all Father LaBrie said was "I'll pick you up tomorrow morning. You'll see."

Last rites, man. You know the end is coming when the local priest is ready to give you your last rites.

* * *

It's too late for me to do the bucket list thing. Wish I could do some traveling—that would be my bucket list. Traveling, man. Looking back, I think traveling has been my greatest joy in life. Problem is, I don't have the strength or the money to travel now. Reading books and watching TV—that's what I do to pass what little time I have left.

Regrets on the travel front—there are some, I'm afraid. On the plus side, I'm thankful to the army for stationing me in Germany and Korea, because those duty stations allowed me to travel around Europe and Asia. Good times, man.

On the downside, I never visited Rome or Paris. I should have visited those cities when I was stationed in Germany, but I was spending too much time drinking beer, taking part in Amsterdam's red-light district, and trying my chances at the poker tables in Monaco. No true regrets, really. I had my fun. I'm not one to get into the would've, could've, should've game. But it would have been fun to visit Rome and Paris.

As for poker, I don't play anymore. I'm too weak, especially after all the chemo rounds I've been through. Yeah, I have a laptop computer here, and on occasion I'll play free poker online, but I get tired fast. I was playing online for a while, then the Department of Justice cracked down on it, and now it's all up in the air. Good ole Big Brother doing his thing. I'm not sure if we live in the freest of countries sometimes.

Of my travels, probably nothing beats Rio de Janeiro. I spent a week there. Fun city. It's like one big red-light district. My trip was during Carnival. Wild, man.

Brazilians know how to party. That was nine years ago. Good times.

It's sad I never got to see the Red Sox play at Fenway. That too would be on my bucket list—to watch a live game at Fenway Park. What an awful season our beloved BoSox had this year. I was excited about Bobby Valentine coming on board, but we never got it going under his reign.

Let me take a sip of hot tea here—mmm. Good stuff. Tea is soothing; warm liquid going down my throat is soothing.

Now, where was I? Yeah, regrets. Well, I never got to see Stevie Ray Vaughan live in concert, but I did see beautiful Austin, Texas, and the live music scene there. It was awesome. Poor Stevie, his life was cut too short. Kinda makes me think of my age. Forty-seven, man. That's too young to call it quits. But then again, the last three years haven't been easy on me. Breathing is tough. Walking is hard. I'm always in pain. Not much energy either. That's what three packs a day will do to you—three packs a day for three decades. It caught up to me, man. Bad habit . . . a bad habit I picked up in the army.

I tried quitting many times, but to no avail. Smoking was a part of me, and I was addicted. I ain't one to blame nobody either, including the tobacco companies. When you think about it, a lot of stuff comes down to math, to probabilities. Smoking cigarettes may not give you cancer, but you're certainly increasing the odds of that happening to you if you keep smoking. I continued smoking, and, in the end, the probability materialized. It's my responsibility, nobody else's. Some heavy smokers don't get cancer, some do. And some nonsmokers also get lung cancer. Genes, lifestyle, diet—they may factor in. It's all probabilities. It's a numbers game, and I lost.

I still smoke, but only two or three cigarettes a day, usually after a meal. I don't have much of an appetite anymore—I mostly eat Campbell's tomato soup and crackers. I used to be a healthy 190 pounds; I now tip the scales at 130. It's all downhill, man.

Back to travels, well . . . lemme see. Panama looked like a nice country from what I could tell, but my vantage point was during combat. It was the invasion of Panama under George Bush the father. That was my first combat experience, my first combat tour. I had four of those in all: Panama, the First Persian Gulf War, then Afghanistan, and Iraq.

The Panamanian conflict proved to be my first and only combat jump. I was airborne infantry back then. Same for the First Persian Gulf War—I was infantry then too, but we didn't jump out of a C-130 in that fight.

Infantry is a young man's game, and when I hit thirty-nine years of age, I changed my army job from infantry to personnel, human resources. My last two deployments— the 'Stan and Iraq—I was doing a desk job, a paper-pushing job, so I had it pretty good. Good A/C, nice mess halls, nice gyms, and Filipino migrant workers doing our laundry. I was a fobbit, stationed at one of the big forward-operating bases (FOBs). Yep, I had it good, man.

Germany was a nice three years in my life. Good sightseeing, great beer, great cars, and Amsterdam, Netherlands, not too far away.

South Korea was a mixed blessing when I think about it. I met my wife there, my now ex-wife, Soon-Bok. The name means gentle and blessed, but she was nothing close to that—more of a selfish, gold-digger type. In fairness, she had some good qualities. She was hardworking, smart, and very beautiful. We were happy in Korea, but everything changed once we came stateside.

"We go to LA, we go to LA, Los Angeles. Please. Please." She kept that request coming, largely in part because she wanted to try her hand at acting, and I—wanting to please—obliged. I requested to be stationed to the nearest post around LA, Fort Irwin, in the middle of nowhere between the City of Angels and Vegas. The army made it happen, so Fort Irwin it was.

We had our good times, but our good times fizzled when Soon-Bok started spending more and more time in Koreatown in Los Angeles. I know her family wasn't crazy about her marrying me. Heck, my parents had mixed feelings too, probably for the same reasons: race and religion. But I thought it could work out, and it didn't. Soon-Bok eventually hooked up with a Korean American dude in LA, and I was relegated to the sidelines. Bottom line, I don't play second fiddle to that shit, so the marriage ended. The big D, divorce. I ended it. She fought tooth and nail with all the legal delays imaginable, but I wouldn't budge.

Soon-Bok figured I was a careerist when it came to the army, so she wanted a slice of my future pension, but I was steadfast in refusing what I thought was an unreasonable demand. I ended up paying her a lump sum of $50,000—well worth it for the peace of mind. She got all the furniture, a relatively new Honda Accord, a new computer, and the diamond ring of course. Me, I got my weight bench, my books, my music CDs, and an old pickup truck. But thankfully I was out of a bad marriage. Sometimes the best way to get rid of a problem is to divorce yourself from it.

In fairness, though, Soon-Bok did give me the very best thing in my life, our daughter, Mi-cah, my pride and joy. Mi-cah is twenty years old, a sophomore at UCLA, and the most important thing in the world to me. Her name means beautiful girl in Korean, and she's definitely that. Beautiful and smart. I'm so proud of her. Maybe I didn't accomplish much in my forty-seven years, but at least I helped raise Mi-cah, and she's turning out real well. In fact, it's time for my daily e-mail to her.

Okay, let me turn on the laptop. There. Type in the good old username and password . . . username . . . Red Sox . . . password . . . Yaztremski. Click enter; click compose.

Dear Mi-cah,

Thank you for your e-mail yesterday. I know I hit you with devastating news two days ago about the spreading of my cancer and the failure of the chemotherapy. I don't want you to worry too much.

Thank you also for sending me a list of oncologists in the LA area, and I appreciate your recommendation that I see them ASAP. I don't think it'll surprise you that, in all likelihood, I won't follow your recommendation, but we can discuss later.

Know that you are the most important thing in my life. I'm so proud of you, Mi-cah. Keep doing that great work at UCLA in your premed studies. Who knows, maybe someday you'll discover a cure for lung cancer. Ha-ha!

On a more serious note—and as we've discussed before—I'm sorry for not always being there in your life. I'm sorry for missing some of your birthdays, but I was in Iraq and

Afghanistan, and I couldn't always take R & R at the time of your special day.

Also, you were not the cause of the divorce between your mother and me. This too we've discussed before, to exhaustion really, but I sometimes feel you're too hard on yourself, and you in part blame yourself for the divorce.

I want you to know I still have my life insurance policy. It used to be SGLI, and now that I'm retired, it's with VGLI. The amount is $400,000, and you are the sole beneficiary. I suspect your mother will inquire about this, fight over it, etc. Bottom line, it is yours. Use it as necessary. Maybe you'll need it to pay for medical school. I don't want you saddled with or burdened by mountains of student loan debts. Early next week, I will give Kevin Nadeau the power of attorney to arrange my affairs. He will also be the executor of my estate. He will have a copy of my life insurance policy.

The love for a child never ends, and so my love for you is ever lasting. I'll call you on Sunday like I normally do, or you can call me first. Until then, be good and safe.

Love always,

Dad

Hit the send button . . . Click logoff . . . There. Okay.

My daughter, man. She does make me so proud.

As for belongings, I don't have much to my name—just clothes, books, a GMC pickup truck, a few hunting rifles, and a baseball card collection.

My brother, Don, will get my hunting rifles. Dad will get my truck. My sister, Paula, will get my baseball card collection. Mom and Dad will get my clothes, which they'll probably donate to charity. All I wear now are sweats—sweatpants and sweatshirts.

It's only fitting that Kevin Nadeau, my best man at my wedding, gets my books. He's a reader, and he dabbles in writing. We often discuss books together. He'll be happy I'm leaving him my small collection. Mi-cah can have the books if she wants, but I doubt she'll want them since she's into vampire and romance novels, genres that never interested me.

I'm looking at my favorite books right now. They're on the small bedside table next to my bed and the small desk: favorites from Michael Crichton and John Grisham, Truman Capote's masterpiece *In Cold Blood*, and Malcolm Gladwell's best sellers along with my favorites by Michael Lewis.

Boy, did Michael Lewis do a great job describing the mess in Greece. Also *Moneyball*, probably the best book on baseball. I'm disappointed Lewis didn't write about the home field advantage (if any) of the Oakland As, but everything else is on point. Next I see Tom Wolfe's *The Bonfire of the Vanities*. I think it's the Great American Novel. There's everything in that book: race, class, North and South, rich and poor, crime and punishment, male-female differences, infidelity and loyalty, race relations, and politics.

I've got the Stieg Larsson best sellers too—true page-turners once you get into them. The Holy Bible is also by my bed even though I'm not big on religion, but maybe I'll get more into it as my final days wind down.

Yesterday Kevin brought me my request: copies of the latest biography of Steve Jobs, the book *Tuesdays with Morrie* by Mitch Albom, *The Last Lecture* by Randy Pausch, and Christopher Hitchens's book about dying entitled *Mortality*. I've read *The Last Lecture* and *Tuesdays with Morrie*, but I just wanted my own copies of them. The Jobs biography I haven't read, nor have I read Hitchens's latest.

I'm a big fan of Christopher Hitchens even if I don't always agree with him. I always looked forward to his articles in *Vanity Fair*. Sad to see him kick the bucket not too long ago. The big C also caught up with him.

Might be joining you soon, Christopher buddy. Doctors say so. Is there an afterlife? I know you were an atheist to the end. If there is an afterlife—the good part called heaven and not the bad part called hell—then I hope you're in heaven and that I end up similarly situated.

The Last Lecture was a good read as I recall. The lesson from Randy Pausch's book is on target: even if you don't achieve everything you set out to, you can help others realize their goals by being a coach or mentor.

Not sure if that lesson applies to me, though. I wasn't much of an achiever. Retiring as a sergeant first class ain't bad, but it reflects that I was always more of a doer than a manager. If I would have pushed myself more, maybe I could have been a master sergeant or a sergeant major, but I pretty much always liked what I was doing, and I was happier working than supervising. Plus, I was often taking college courses during my army career to obtain my bachelor's degree in history. I finally did get my degree from the University of Maryland, but it took me almost seven years to realize that goal. Looking back, the time I spent pursuing my degree might have been put to better career-enhancement use if I would have done more military schools, such as ranger school or drill sergeant school. Still, I did what I liked, and I had my fun. No regrets—no would'ves, could'ves, should'ves.

Mitch Albom did some good writing in *Tuesdays with Morrie*. There were good parts in that book, but there were disappointments too. I couldn't get myself to agree with Morrie all the time. He was so much against consumerism and capitalism. Working hard and getting ahead in life were like cardinal sins to him. Me, I feel bad I haven't accumulated a lot in my life. What's wrong with working hard and buying stuff? True, in the end, family and friendships are probably the most important things, but there's nothing wrong with working hard and accumulating stuff.

I think Morrie saw the rat race as bad, but what if you like your work? I always liked my job and my various army postings. I would have stayed infantry if I could, but it's a young man's game, and I wasn't young anymore; jumping out of planes was taking its toll on my back and knees and ankles. I switched to human resources, and that was fun work too.

I regret I never wrote a book. I have the energy to type e-mails, but that's about it; I simply don't have the energy, concentration, and focus to write a book. I always wanted to write a novel loosely based on my infantry days in Germany, sort of a Tom Clancyish type of book. Clancy is another one of my favorite writers, but all of my Clancy books are gone now. They were in my apartment at Fort Irwin, but the ex-wife cleaned house before I could do anything. We were going through a messy divorce, and I kept asking her where my Clancy books were. She kept denying she took them. Maybe Hemingway was right: a bitch is a bitch is a bitch.

Stephen King, a fellow Mainer, was always my biggest inspiration to write a book. His book *On Writing* is awesome. I'm not a big fan of his horror genre, but I always thought his novellas *Apt Pupil* and *Rita Hayworth and Shawshank Redemption* were exceptional.

Okay, time for some more tea. Lemme get another Lipton tea bag here . . . Pour some hot water in my cup . . . There. Good stuff.

Back to writers, my favorite one is Michael Crichton, because he was always able to combine entertainment with a lesson; I always felt I learned something after reading a Crichton novel.

Truman Capote—he's the best writer I ever read. Saul Bellow is another good one, but no one beats Capote. Hemingway is up there too. With Capote, I don't care what the subject is—I don't care what I'm reading— because the writing is so beautiful: long sentences, unlike the Hemingway style, but beautiful sentences indeed. Jack London was another great one. Grisham is always entertaining, as is James Patterson. Hitchens was great as well. In my opinion, the only guy who could hold his own against Hitchens debate-wise was Dinesh D'Souza. Of course I'll read Hitchens's *Mortality*. I look forward to it. I just need to gather the energy to read. I'll probably start on it this weekend.

Someone's knocking at my door.

"Yes, who is it?" I ask.

"Glenn, it's me. Kevin. Open up, buddy."

"Ah, Kevin. Just a minute. I ain't as fast as I used to be, slugger."

Man, just this short walk of no more than ten feet is hard, exhausting. Um, let me open this door. There.

"Hey, c'mon in," I say.

"You're looking good, buddy," Kevin says. "Always wearing those sweats I see."

"Thanks, but don't sugarcoat it. I'm weak, have little to no appetite, and my hair is just starting to grow back. I know I don't look good. Have a seat."

"Okay."

"Want anything to drink? Water? Tea? I'm sorry I don't have coffee or soda, but I don't drink that stuff."

"Nah, I'm good, and I won't be long. Wife wants to go out to eat tonight, and I have to get an oil change before that at Daigle GMC."

"Understood."

"Here, I brought you something. It's John Grisham's latest. I should have given you this yesterday when I brought those other books," Kevin says.

"Thanks. I appreciate it."

"No problem. I ordered all the books on Amazon. Isn't Amazon great?"

"Sure is. Amazon has definitely leveled the playing field. Small towns like Frenchville can get all these books now."

"That's right."

"Well, Kev, like I told you yesterday, doctors say I ain't got much time to live. It's terminal. I want you to be the executor of my will."

"Okay. Sure. Anything for you, man."

"My parents could do the job—bless their hearts—but I'd rather have you do it. My family won't complain. And they won't fight over stuff either. Ex-wife might, though. That's really why I prefer you as the executor."

"Okay. By the way, don't give up, man. You know there are experimental drugs in Mexico and stuff. Keep fighting the good fight. Doctors get it wrong sometimes."

"Yeah, the reality is I'm tired. Chemo rounds have taken their toll on me. I'm weak and tired. Maybe it's time this former soldier hangs it up and calls it quits."

"Never knew you to be a quitter, dude. I'm telling you, there are experimental cancer drugs in Mexico and Thailand and places like that. I've done some surfing on the web."

"Well, we can discuss that later. Anyway, next week I want you to take me to Bruce Blanchette's law office to finalize my will."

"Sure thing. Too easy," Kevin says.

"Pretty much everything I own is in this small room except for my pickup truck and rifles. I want my dad to get my pickup truck."

"Sounds like a plan."

"My parents can keep my clothes. I know they'll give them to charity. I want my baseball card collection to go to Paula. She lives in the DC area, northern Virginia. You'll have her address."

"How's Paula doing, by the way?" Kevin asks. "You were always close to your sister."

"Doing great. Married a good guy. They own a printing franchise. Business is steady." I take another sip of tea. "I want Don to get my hunting rifles."

"Okay. And how's he doing? Your brother was always a character."

"Doing well as a commercial fisherman in Alaska. He loves it up there. Found himself a nice girlfriend too. She's a Native woman. A real hottie, I might add."

"Oh yeah, Don always had an eye for the girls, didn't he?"

"Sure did. And uh . . . I want my photo albums to be split between my daughter, Mi-cah, and my mom."

"Sure, Glenn. No worries. I'll see to it. I still think you can beat this cancer thing and—"

"Well, we can discuss that another time," I interrupt. "The big thing is I've got a life insurance policy. That too will be copied at Mr. Blanchette's law office. The beneficiary is Mi-cah."

"She's still in LA?"

"Yes, at UCLA. She gets all of my life insurance."

"Okay."

"And I was thinking of my pallbearers."

"Ah, man, don't think that way. I'm telling you, they got experimental cancer drugs in Mexico and—"

"I know, I know, but I need to plan for worst-case shit. Anyway, I was thinking of Joel Michaud, Mike Dionne, Rodney Gervais, Tom Gagnon, David Voisine, and Keith Daigle for pallbearers and—"

"Uh, Tom Gagnon's in jail, county jail in Houlton. He was dealing pot. Not sure when he gets out. And David Voisine moved to Connecticut last month. Got a welding job there."

"Okay, well, as backups, how about Allan Corriveau and Brian Boucher?" I say.

"That'll probably work."

"You can be a pallbearer too if need be but—"

"Ah, don't talk that way, man. Don't talk that shit. I really think you should consider going to Mexico to—"

"I know. Listen, if I kick the bucket, that's who I want as pallbearers."

"Okay." Kevin nods.

"At my funeral, I want to be in my class A military uniform."

"Okay."

"And I want full military honors. I'm entitled to that. Twenty-one-gun salute, the folding of the flag, and the playing of taps. I think the local National Guard unit has a funeral detail. Mike Dionne is in that unit. Get with him to ensure that happens."

"Will do."

"That's about it," I say.

"How are your parents with all of this?"

"Well, they're hanging in there, I guess. They want to cancel their annual snowbird migration to Florida, but I'm trying to talk them out of it."

"Good luck with that. Your parents have been spending winters in Florida for what, five years now?"

"Yeah, something like that. I don't think I'll be able to talk them out of it. Anyway, they're doing okay considering."

"Good."

"Of course they don't know that earlier today Father LaBrie visited me and said he wanted to administer my last rites tomorrow. He told me we can do confession too, if I want."

"Shit, Glenn. I haven't been to confession in ages."

"Same here. And you know what else? Father LaBrie told me he wants to take me for a ride before he administers the last rites."

"Hmm . . . a ride? Where to?"

"Don't know. I asked him the same thing. He just said he wants to take me for a ride somewhere."

"Well, he's a personable fellow. Good priest. Down to earth. Drinks beer and smokes cigarettes like many of us. A ride, huh? What's that all about?" Kevin asks.

"Beats me."

"Well, Father LaBrie probably wants to go over a few things. I know he also likes to drive his Ford Explorer, you know."

"Yeah, that's what I hear. Anyway, that'll be tomorrow. Oh, and by the way, I'd like you to give my eulogy. My parents and siblings will probably want to say a few things, but I want you to give the eulogy."

"Dude, I'm telling you, don't give up. Fight the good fight. I see the portable oxygen tank next to you, and I know that you're weak and still bald from all the chemo shit, but I'm telling you, there are experimental cancer drugs in Mexico that aren't available here and—"

"I know, I know. Maybe I'll consider that. But I've got to plan for the worst, buddy."

"Well . . . all right. I'd be honored to give the eulogy."

"Oh, and, Kev, it'll be in my will—you get my books."

"Shit, for the past twenty years, you've been sending me books as gifts for the holidays. I always looked forward to getting those books from you."

"It was my pleasure. Do you know what you'll say about me for the eulogy?"

"Oh, I'll come up with something, but I'd prefer researching cancer drugs on Google."

"I know, but you're okay with it? The eulogy?"

"Yeah. If it comes to that, I'll have nice things to say. Just say it like it is, right? Glenn Greenwood/Gilles Boisvert. Baseball, some fishing and hunting, picking potatoes, chasing chicks with the best of them, army soldier, combat veteran, lover of books."

"Sounds good, dude," I say.

"Loving father too. I'll mention that. Mi-cah's lucky to have you as a father."

"Thanks, Kev."

"You know, this reminds me about something I heard not too long ago on C-SPAN."

"What's that?" I ask.

"Brian Lamb was interviewing Morley Safer, one of the reporters/newscasters for *60 Minutes,* and Safer said Don Hewitt always reminded the staff, 'We don't cover issues;

we tell stories.' I think that's how I would eulogize you—by telling stories."

"Okay, if that's what works."

"Sure are plenty of stories on you, eh?"

"Well, I guess."

"Remember when we lost the Valley Little League championship two years in a row to the Madawaska Red Sox? Always down to the wire, always down to the last inning."

"Oh yeah."

"We could never put them away."

"That's right," I say.

"I'll have some Little League baseball stories."

"Good. I figured you would."

"Also high school baseball. Remember when Moose pitched a two-hitter against our nemesis, the Washburn Beavers?"

"Oh yeah. Moose had it going."

"And remember in soccer when Coach Beaulieu got ejected from the game in Mars Hill for arguing a call?" Kevin asks.

"Oh yeah."

"How often do you see that? How often does a soccer coach get ejected from a game?"

"Beats me," I say. "Good memories, man."

"Yeah, and Coach Beaulieu turned to you, our starting striker, and said, 'Gilles, coach this game. I'm out. You're a player-coach now.'"

"Oh yeah."

"How often do you see a player-coach in high school soccer?"

"Yeah, good memories," I say.

"And remember when we were picking potatoes for Luc Lavoie, and during lunch break, Kim Dufour wanted to show us her tits, but we were too nervous?"

"Oh yeah, crazy stuff. You won't tell that story at my funeral, right?"

"Nah, I'll keep it clean, but I'd sure like to talk about the time a bunch of us went to Bar 185, and we took Steve Roy with us because he wanted to be a priest after high school; he wanted to go to the seminary."

"I'll never forget it. Nothing like bringing a future Catholic priest to the local strip joint to show him what he's giving up."

"Well, listen, buddy, I gotta head out. I'll swing by on Monday," Kevin says.

"Sounds like a plan. Send my best to Linda."

"Will do. Later."

*   *   *

Kevin, man. He's a good chap, a dear friend. He works at the local paper mill, and he's a devoted husband and father. He reminds me of John Belushi. Looks a bit like him too. I remember watching a Dan Aykroyd interview where he was asked, "Mr. Aykroyd, tell us about John

Belushi," and Aykroyd responded, "Ah, John Belushi—a good man, but a bad boy." Kevin's like that, man.

*   *   *

Hell, man, the big C announcement came three days ago, this past Tuesday, on Election Day of all days. Even with the bad news, I still went to the polls and voted.

I voted for Romney. I stayed up till eleven thirty that night still not knowing who had won the election. Wednesday morning I woke up and turned on my laptop. I saw that President Obama won a second and final term.

I've got good things to say about President Obama, but I thought Romney would make a better president. Obama deserves good marks on the raid and killing of Osama Bin Laden. Good mission, well executed too. President Bush deserves some credit on that one as well, but Obama was the one who had to make the call, and he did it right.

Though I didn't vote for Obama in 2008, I like the fact the race issue is no longer in play for the American presidency. Personally, I always thought Colin Powell would be America's first black president, but he chose not to run, and—

There's another knock on the door.

"Yes? Who is it?" I ask.

"It's me, dear."

"Oh, hi, Mom. Let me get the door. Just a moment . . . There."

"Oh, dear, how are you? I brought you some soup. It's still warm, just the way you like it."

"Thanks."

"Let me get you a spoon. This cupboard, right?"

"Right. But I'm not all that hungry right now, but thanks for—"

"You need to eat, dear," my mother interrupts, walking past me to get a spoon. "You know, your father and I have been thinking a lot, and we think you should get another opinion about the cancer. There are good doctors in Bangor and Portland. Your father and I could drive you and—"

"Yeah, thanks. We can discuss that later."

"Yes, well, it's no trouble at all for us, dear. We're not going to Florida this winter. Your father figures we can rent our condo for a thousand dollars a month, so we'll make a bit of money on it."

"You guys should go to Florida like you normally do," I say. "And please, sit down."

"Okay, but don't argue, Gilles. You're weak, but we can maybe get the cancer out. Here, have some soup."

"I'm not hungry right now. I'll have some later."

"I crushed some of the saltine crackers you like. They're already soaking in the soup."

"That's great. Thanks. I'll have it later."

"Your father's a wreck from all of this, you know."

"Yeah."

"He keeps talking about the good memories. Bringing you and Don and Paula out for hot dogs and ployes at Rock's in Fort Kent; paying for your first beer at Bee-Jays. He keeps saying, 'Seems like just yesterday I was taking the kids out for hot dogs or Little League or fishing.'"

"Yeah, poor Dad."

"Now have you told Don and Paula yet? I haven't because it should come from you first, but they call every Sunday and I'll have to say something. I know they know about the cancer, but have you told them what the doctor said this week?"

"Uh, no," I say. "I haven't told Don and Paula that my cancer's terminal. I'll let them know soon, probably tonight in an e-mail."

"You should see other doctors. It's always a good idea to get other opinions. Your father and I can drive you down to Bangor or Portland and—"

"Thanks, but let me think about it." I sit back in my chair, my old rocker.

"Now your father and I will be going to Mass Sunday. Are you too weak to attend Mass, dear?"

"Yeah, I think so. I didn't go last week."

"Well, I know Father LaBrie gives Mass at this nursing home too. On Saturdays, late afternoon, right? You shouldn't miss Mass."

"Yes, Mom. I'll do my best to attend Mass. And yes, Mass here is held Saturday in the late afternoon."

"You know, I bumped into Father LaBrie at Dave's Gas yesterday. He said he knew about your diagnosis and that he was saying prayers. He told me he would visit you. Has he come to visit you yet?" my mom asks.

"Yes, he has."

"Well, that's nice of him. He's such a good priest. I figure one of the many nurses at the Fort Kent hospital told him about your cancer. You know he gives Mass there, too."

"Yes, I know."

"News travels so fast here in the small towns of the Valley."

"Yeah, it does."

"Please have some soup, dear. You need to eat. Cancer is fightable, you know. Doctors gave Eddie Gagnon a year to live, and he's going on year four."

"Yes, Mom. I'm just not hungry right now."

"I can bring you a list of the Portland doctors on Monday."

"Okay, that would be fine."

"Well, I've got to go make supper for your father. Call me on Sunday, dear, after you talk to Don and Paula."

"Okay, sounds like a plan. Love ya."

"I love you too, dear."

She hugs me and then leaves my room.

*   *   *

I have great parents. They raised us right, did everything for us. It's sad to think of dying before they do. I really don't want to die, but I don't want to suffer either, and my condition ain't getting any better. These last three years have been a rapid decline. I know my body, and it don't feel right. I'm gonna fight the good fight, but I feel the end coming.

*   *   *

Sipping tea here, thinking about my favorites. Let's see . . . favorite writer—Michael Crichton; favorite book—*Travels* by Michael Crichton; favorite food—pizza, deep dish, Chicago style; favorite beer—Sam Adams; favorite music—Stevie Ray Vaughan.

The best day of my life was about ten years ago. I was stationed at Fort Drum, New York, and I was dating a gorgeous Filipina sergeant, Sabrina Santos. We weren't in the same unit, so we could date. It was a Saturday in July, and we decided to drive down to Cooperstown to visit the Baseball Hall of Fame. It was a beautiful summer day. I remember we stopped for ice cream along the way, some ice cream parlor out in the middle of the woods. Once we arrived at the Hall of Fame, we spent hours there. God, it was gorgeous. I read up on my favorite players: Johnny Bench, Mickey Mantle, Babe Ruth, and Ted Williams. After spending hours in the museum, we went outside and saw a baseball game at a beautiful baseball field in Cooperstown. It was a men's league, with middle-aged guys still playing the game they loved. Dusk was approaching, but it was still nice out. It was so beautiful, so picturesque. It was like something out of a Norman Rockwell painting: sunset and a bunch of guys playing our nation's pastime.

Sabrina and I decided to get a hotel room and stay overnight. We drank beer and watched TV and made love all night long. Gosh, she was beautiful, and fun.

I had a good thing going with Sabrina, but then our nation's wars in the Middle East separated us—her unit deployed to Iraq while mine headed to Afghanistan. We kept in touch via e-mail and Skype, but then one day she told me she had another man in her life, and that was that.

*   *   *

SATURDAY

I had a good shower and shave this morning. Even those simple tasks take a lot out of me, but this morning wasn't so bad. Rocking in my rocking chair right now, sipping some tea. Got Fox News on the television. I'm just waiting for Father LaBrie.

News programs can be quite depressing at times. Fiscal cliff, global warming, war in Syria, an unpredictable Iran, threat of another recession, General Petraeus stepping down as CIA director.

There's rarely any good news out there. I think the media are prone to negativity and making a mountain out of a molehill. Exaggeration seems to be a part of their business model; it gives them a sense of importance. C-SPAN is the best network for news coverage. I think it has the best format: cover news, interview experts, and discuss the issues in depth.

One C-SPAN pet peeve of mine, however, is when the program allows for viewers to call in and ask questions. Sometimes the questions are on point, but I often find it's better just to listen to the interviewee/expert on the topic, especially since callers often make a comment instead of asking a question.

The dominant story right now is Hurricane Sandy, and I of course feel bad for the loss of life and for the people who are still without electricity. I'm not convinced such a hurricane has anything to do with global warming and climate change—the news media feed us that angle, but I think history will prove this line of thinking wrong.

* * *

I hear a knock on my door.

"Yes, who is it?" I ask.

"Good morning, Glenn. It's me, Father LaBrie."

I struggle a bit to get up, and I open the door for him.

"Good morning, Father. Would you like some tea?"

"No, that's okay. I already had my morning coffee. I'm fine. Thanks anyway."

Father LaBrie looks good for his age. I found out he's sixty-three, but he looks maybe fifty, no more than fifty-five. I heard he was a good hockey player in his day. He's almost six feet tall, probably two hundred pounds. Receding hairline with touches of gray on the sides.

"Well, let's go for that ride I told you about," he says. "Do you need help with your oxygen tank?"

"No, I'm fine, Father. It rolls easily."

I'm dressed in sweats. I struggle to put on my hooded sweater, and Father LaBrie helps me out.

Father LaBrie is wearing a black shirt and black pants befitting a Catholic priest. He's also wearing a thick, dark gray overcoat. His glasses are of the thin-framed variety. I only need glasses to read, so I won't bring them for this ride. We exit my room of the nursing home and head out to Father LaBrie's Ford Explorer. I'm pulling my oxygen tank along.

"Here, let me open the passenger door for you . . . There," Father LaBrie says.

"Thank you."

"There'll be room for your oxygen tank right here on the front seat."

"Yes, that'll do. Thank you," I say.

I climb into the Explorer and place my small oxygen tank apparatus to my left on the front seat. Father LaBrie starts the Explorer and quickly pulls out of the nursing home parking lot.

"Glenn, I've decided to bring you up to the Desjardin Farm. You know, the one about five miles from here on Church Road."

"Yes, I know it." *This is weird—the Desjardin Farm. Hmm.*

Father LaBrie navigates the curves of US Route 1—Frenchville's main road—at a speed of around forty miles per hour. In no time we reach Church Road, and he takes a left, heading uphill toward Frenchville's back settlements.

The Desjardin Farm. Hmm.

"I've checked all your records," Father LaBrie says, "and you did receive the sacraments of baptism, Communion, and confirmation."

"Correct. All here at St. Luce Parish."

"Those are prerequisites for receiving your last rites."

"Understood, Father."

Father LaBrie is now driving at a speed hovering around fifty miles per hour. To my right, I see the small creek where Don and I used to fish. To the left are potato fields, recently harvested.

"I'm sorry, of course, to hear about your cancer." Father LaBrie's voice is calm, serious, and direct. "My prayers are with you."

"Thank you, Father."

I keep thinking about the Desjardin Farm and its significance.

After more curves and hills, we reach the back settlements, the area where the hills and woods make way for flat fields and a plateau. The sight makes me think back to the days when we students were let out of school for three weeks in mid-September to early October to pick potatoes. My best day was sixty-eight barrels. I was picking russet potatoes. Kevin picked seventy barrels that day and won the gentleman's bet between us. We were paid thirty-five cents a barrel.

I see the Desjardin Farm ahead.

More driving, more curves and turns, but no hills now.

Father LaBrie slows down the Explorer and takes a right turn on a small, narrow dirt road. A large barn, bright red in color, is to our left. The heavy tree line of poplars and firs is to our right, maybe one hundred yards away. A large, recently harvested potato field is directly in front of us. I put it at sixty acres.

I remember picking potatoes here for the Bergeron Farm that Mr. Desjardin eventually bought out. I also remember the time, during our lunch break, when a huge bull moose came trotting out of the wood line. Kevin threw a small potato at it, but the moose just kept on trotting as if nothing bothered it. I'm guessing the moose came within fifty yards of us, and then it just stared at us for a long time. It finally trotted back into the woods, impervious to humans.

"Why are we here, Father?" I finally ask.

"Glenn," he tells me without making eye contact, "there's someone I want you to meet."

"Someone? Who?"

"You'll see shortly." His tone is calm.

The Explorer comes to a stop next to the barn and I get out. I leave my oxygen-assistance tank in the truck. The air is cool, especially with the breeze. I'm guessing the temperature is in the low forties.

Father LaBrie walks forward, toward the edge of the barn. I follow him with the slow walk that I can muster. We pass the edge of the barn, and suddenly, to our left, a woman gets out of an old, faded yellow Volkswagen Bug. I had noticed the car briefly from nearly a quarter mile away, but I thought nothing of it, even though a car like that sticks out like a sore thumb around here. This is GM and Ford country, with imported cars being the rare exception to the norm. I figured it might be college kids from Fort Kent smoking pot or making out or something. I notice the car's Connecticut license plate, dark blue with white lettering. The woman walks toward us. I stop walking.

Tina Plourde is my former high school sweetheart and senior prom date. Tina has colored her hair blonde. She's put on some weight, but she still looks great. Father LaBrie is standing next to me.

I know what this is about.

Tina walks up to me. She's in jeans, a beige sweater, and a brown leather jacket. Her beautiful face is sad. My heart beats faster. I too am sad. Father LaBrie is quiet; his head is down.

"We were young, Glenn," she says. "I almost called you Gilles, but I found out about your name change." She smiles and that comforts me some. "I was visiting relatives when I happened to see Father LaBrie on Wednesday. He told me about your cancer. I'm sorry to hear about that."

I manage to say thanks.

"I confessed to him," Tina says. "I confessed to Father LaBrie on Wednesday. No grand design, it wasn't planned, but I thought it was the right thing to do and the right time to do it. You too should confess."

I don't have the nerve to look at Father LaBrie. I don't feel mad or confused or tricked or duped—nothing like that. I only have one feeling: sadness. I'm sad.

"We were young, Glenn."

Some thirty years ago, during my senior year in high school, I was dating Tina. Our courtship started around Christmastime. Winter and basketball season were upon us—I, the starting point guard; she, a beautiful brunette on the cheerleading squad. Then came spring and baseball, then the senior prom, and then graduation. I knew I was heading to army boot camp in the fall, and that Tina and her family were moving to Connecticut around the same time, her father landing a better job there.

Tina accidentally became pregnant, accidentally in that it wasn't planned, of course. We figured it was around prom night—not prom night itself but a bit afterward.

The prom was fun. We were carefree then. No scoring, but we messed around, feeling each other out. Later— maybe a week or so afterward—one thing led to another, and it wasn't too long after that when Tina told me she was pregnant.

I'm a let's-work-it-out type of person: let's have the child, the army will work out, and we'll get free health care through the army. That was my thinking, my perspective, my hope really. Get married and have the child. Things will work out.

But Tina wanted none of that. Our relationship, in her mind, was a fling. Now she was pregnant, and her family was moving to Connecticut. She didn't want a child, and she didn't want to get married.

"Okay, I'll raise the child," I remember telling her, but that fell on deaf ears. She had other plans, and a child and marrying me were not part of them. To my understanding, no one knew of the pregnancy except Tina and me. I certainly didn't tell anyone, nor did Tina, to my knowledge. In the end, Tina's desires were clear: no child and no marriage; she wanted an abortion.

Frenchville is a small town surrounded by small towns. Everybody knows everybody. We were in a tough bind. Carrying the child to term came with the scarlet-letter treatment—a child born out of wedlock is rare around here, and when it does happen, it's looked down upon. Another option was giving the child up for adoption, but Tina didn't want that. She wanted an abortion. I was steadfast against abortion, but Tina was determined to have one. I couldn't stop her, and so I decided to help her out.

Tina's plan was for her to perform the abortion herself with me serving as a lookout. Abortions just don't happen around here; we knew of no doctors who performed them. The plan was for the abortion to take place right here— right here behind the huge Desjardin Farm barn with little chance that anyone would see us and discover our doings. Tina's plan was simple: she would stuff a twig inside her while I stood at the edge of the barn to ensure no traffic was heading this way.

Tina squatted behind the barn. It was a warm day in August. I couldn't look. I've hunted before and seen chickens get beheaded. I've skinned rabbits, seen pigs get slaughtered. But this I couldn't watch. Besides, my job in the plan was to check for the possibility of any traffic or onlookers.

I prayed and prayed. I started crying when I heard Tina's soft grunts and cries. I was scared. I prayed to Jesus and to Mary. An abortion. It happened. No proper burial, just Tina with a shovel, digging a small grave and placing the remains in it. I couldn't watch any of it. I never knew the gender of the fetus-child.

I was the one who drove Tina to the Desjardin Farm barn in my dad's pickup truck. I served as a lookout, and after it was done, I drove her back to her home, both of us crying along the way. Then she moved to Connecticut, and I joined the army. The transgressions of youth.

Dear Lord, forgive me.

Tina and I wrote letters for some time, but that faded and eventually died altogether. This was before the Internet and e-mail.

Over the years, I did keep in touch with friends, particularly Kevin, and I came to discover that Tina had gone on to college and eventually law school, that she was married and had two sons, and that she was a successful family-law attorney. All of that was great news, helping to erase our secret deed.

Tina approaches me. She's sad and she's crying softly. I too am sad. My lips tremble. I feel warm tears rolling down my cheeks.

"I felt better confessing to Father LaBrie," she tells me.

I swallow hard. "Father LaBrie," I say, my voice shaky and weak. I feel more warm tears rolling down my cheeks. "Father, I have something to confess. But I'd like my last rites and final confession to be administered back at the nursing home."

AUTHOR'S NOTE

When writing about a controversial subject like abortion, readers may wonder where exactly the writer stands on this issue. The answer in my case is that I'm pro-life.

I believe life is the most precious thing we have; I believe innocent life needs to be protected. I also believe abortion is warranted in cases of rape, incest, or when the health and/or life of the mother carrying the child is at issue. My views are consistent with the pro-life position, although some purist pro-lifers (those who believe abortion is never warranted) may disagree.

Having grown up in the small town of Frenchville—the setting of this short story—I feel the need to emphasize

Last Rites: Final Confession is a work of fiction. Though some of the establishments and references mentioned in the story are true (Bar 185, Bee-Jays, and Church Road, for example, did exist during my childhood), none of the names or characters are real. *Last Rites: Final Confession* is not a true story or loosely based on one. It is a work of fiction.

Paul Bouchard
Laurel, Maryland
March 2013